Trouble for Grandpa

ROB LEWIS

RED FOX

A Red Fox Book

Published by Random House Children's Books
20 Vauxhall Bridge Road, London SW1V 2SA

A division of Random House UK Ltd
London Melbourne Sydney Auckland
Johannesburg and agencies throughout the world

Copyright © Rob Lewis 1997

3 5 7 9 10 8 6 4 2

First published in Great Britain by Red Fox 1997

Printed in Hong Kong

RANDOM HOUSE UK Limited Reg. No. 954009

ISBN 0 09 921872 0

ELVIS

Finley sat in Grandpa's best chair.
They were watching sport on the
television.
It was their favourite programme.
'What would you like for supper?'
asked Grandpa.
'Hot dogs please,' said Finley.
'You always want hot dogs,' said
Grandpa.
'They're my favourite,' said Finley.
After supper Grandpa and Finley went
for a drive.

Grandpa's car was very old.

It didn't even have a roof.

Finley liked it very much.

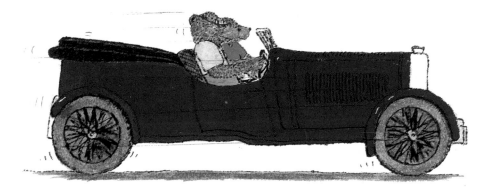

A cat crossed the road in front of
the car.

'I'm getting a cat,' said Grandpa.

'You are too busy for pets,' said Finley.

'Cats are no trouble,' said Grandpa.

Finley went to Grandpa's house the next week.

'This is Elvis,' said Grandpa.

'Hello,' said Finley.

'HSSSSS!' said Elvis.

'He is very friendly,' said Grandpa.

'He doesn't *look* friendly,' said Finley.

Elvis went into the living room.

He sat on the best chair.

'That's *my* chair,' said Finley, crossly.

'HSSSSs!'

said Elvis.

'Elvis likes that chair,' said Grandpa.

Finley sat on the floor. It was time for

their favourite television programme.

'HSSSSS!'

said Elvis.

'Elvis doesn't like sport,' said Grandpa.
'Let's have supper instead.'

Elvis sat at the table with Grandpa
and Finley.

'Can I have hot dogs again?' asked
Finley.

'No,' said Grandpa. 'Elvis doesn't like
hot dogs. We are having fish.'

'Oh,' said Finley.

He didn't like fish much.

After tea Grandpa and Finley washed
the dishes.

'Can we go for a drive now?'
asked Finley.

'Not this evening,' said Grandpa.

'Elvis needs his worming pills.'

'That won't take long,' said Finley.

'It will,' said Grandpa.

'Elvis doesn't like worming pills.'

Finley went home.

Visiting Grandpa wasn't fun with
Elvis there.

But the next week Elvis had gone.

'Cats are too much trouble,' said
Grandpa.

'Good!' smiled Finley.

'And Mavis doesn't like cats,' added
Grandpa.

'Who is Mavis?' asked Finley.

'My new girlfriend,' said Grandpa, proudly.

Finley's eyes opened very wide.

'Grandpas don't have girlfriends,' he said.

'Girlfriends are no trouble,' grinned Grandpa.

'Hello!' said Mavis.

'Hello,' said Finley.

They went into the living room.

Mavis sat in the best chair.

Finley turned
on the television.

'Oh good!' said Mavis.

'*Crimebusters* is on.'

'I was going to watch the sport,'
said Finley.

'Mavis doesn't like sport,' said Grandpa.

After *Crimebusters* they had supper.

'Are we having hot dogs?' Finley

asked, hopefully.

Mavis made a face.

'Mavis doesn't eat meat,' said Grandpa.

'She is a vegetarian.'

'Does she eat fish?' asked Finley.

'No,' said Grandpa. 'Only vegetables.'

'That's a relief,' said Finley.

'We are having parsnip stew,' said
Grandpa. Finley didn't like parsnip
stew much either.

After supper Grandpa and Finley
washed the dishes.

'Can we go for a drive?' asked Finley.

'Mavis doesn't like drives,' said Grandpa, sadly. 'They make her car-sick.'

'Mavis is less fun than Elvis!' grumbled Finley. 'I bet she takes worming pills too!'

'Don't be silly,' said Grandpa.

'Pass me my pills, dear!'

called Mavis.
Grandpa gave Finley a funny look.

20

SHELF TROUBLE

Grandpa and Finley were visiting
Mavis.

Mavis stomped about in the kitchen.
Then she clattered the dishes.

'Uh oh!' said Finley. 'Mavis is in a bad
mood.'

'It must be the weather,' said Grandpa.

Mavis had a headache. She went
upstairs for a rest.

'We will have to cheer her up,'
said Finley.

'We could do the dishes,' suggested
Grandpa.

'Dishes are no fun,' said Finley.

'We could hang out the washing,'
said Grandpa.

'It's raining outside,' said Finley.

'We could vacuum the living room,'
said Grandpa.

'It will make too much noise,'
said Finley.

Grandpa and Finley thought for a long time. They went into the kitchen to make a drink.

Then Grandpa had an idea.
'We could put up some shelves,' he said.

'Won't that make a lot of noise?'
asked Finley.

'Not if I hammer quietly,' said Grandpa.

Grandpa got some tools from the shed.

He drilled holes and hammered quietly. He had to do a lot of hammering and drilling before the shelves looked straight.

'What about the other holes?' Finley asked. 'We'll use some filler,' said Grandpa.

Grandpa found some filler under the sink.

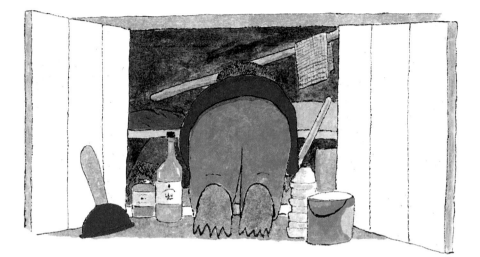

He put the powder in a bowl and added some water.

He mixed it with an electric mixer.

The filler sprayed around the room.

'I think the speed is too fast,' said
Grandpa.

Grandpa gave up with the filler.

'I will pick some flowers for Mavis,' he said. 'Then she won't mind the mess.'

Finley was not so sure.

He filled in some holes while Grandpa picked flowers.

When Grandpa came back they heard
a noise upstairs.

'Mavis is awake,' said Grandpa.

'I must go now,' said Finley.

'I have homework to do.'

Finley hurried down the road.

He heard a loud noise from Mavis's
house.

'Aaaaaah!'

A few days later, Finley met Grandpa
in the street.

He was carrying a big box.

'Where is Mavis?' asked Finley.

'Mavis has gone,' said Grandpa.

'Good,' said Finley. 'Girlfriends are too much trouble.'

'You're right,' said Grandpa.

'And Mavis wouldn't like Conan ...'

Grandpa lifted the lid of the box.

'Uh oh!' said Finley.

CONAN

Finley was looking at Conan.

'Conan is a very big bird,' he said.

'Yes,' said Grandpa, proudly. 'And he does tricks.'

'Really?' said Finley.

'He can ruffle his feathers,' said Grandpa.

Conan ruffled his feathers.

'That's not clever,' said Finley.
'He can hang upside down,'
said Grandpa.

Conan hung upside down.
'Not bad,' said Finley.
'And he can add!' said Grandpa.
'You're joking,' said Finley.
'Watch,' said Grandpa.

'Conan, what is three plus three?'

'Aark aark aark aark aark aark,'

said Conan.

'That *is* clever!' said Finley.

'I will be famous,' boasted Grandpa.

'Conan will be famous, you mean,'
said Finley.

Grandpa told his neighbour, Fred,
about Conan.

He told the cashier at
the supermarket.

He even told people at the bus stop.

On Monday Fred came to see Conan.
'The newspaper will be interested,'
he said.

On Tuesday a reporter came.
He asked Grandpa a lot of questions.
He asked Conan a lot of sums.
'He is a very clever bird,'
said the reporter.

On Wednesday, there were a a lot of reporters at the door.

They wanted pictures of Grandpa.

They wanted pictures of Conan.

They wanted pictures of Grandpa and Conan together.

The reporters asked him questions all day. Grandpa was very tired.

On Thursday the television crew came. They filmed Grandpa and Conan all day.

'This is too much!' Grandpa said.

On Friday he took Conan back to the shop.

Finley visited Grandpa in the evening.

'Where is Conan?' asked Finley.

'On the television,' said Grandpa.

They watched Conan on the television.

'What is six take away two?' said the man.

'Aark aark aark aark,'

said Conan.

Everybody clapped.

'Birds are too much trouble,' said
Grandpa. 'Now I just have a hamster.'
'Can it do tricks?' asked Finley.
'No,' said Grandpa.
'That's good,' said Finley.

'I can talk!'

said the hamster.

'Uh oh!' said Grandpa and Finley.